A Visit to Amy-Claire

A Visit to Amy-Claire

CLAUDIA MILLS

ILLUSTRATED BY SHEILA HAMANAKA

Macmillan Publishing Company   *New York*

Maxwell Macmillan Canada   *Toronto*
Maxwell Macmillan International   *New York   Oxford   Singapore   Sydney*

Macmillan Publishing Company is part of the
Maxwell Communication Group of Companies.

Macmillan Publishing Company
866 Third Avenue
New York, NY 10022

Maxwell Macmillan Canada, Inc.
1200 Eglinton Avenue East
Suite 200
Don Mills, Ontario M3C 3N1

First Edition
Printed in Hong Kong

10 9 8 7 6 5 4 3 2 1

The text of this book is set in 15 pt. ITC Garamond Book.
The illustrations are rendered in oil on canvas.

Library of Congress Cataloging-in-Publication Data
Mills, Claudia. A visit to Amy-Claire / Claudia Mills ; illustrated by
Sheila Hamanaka.   p.   cm. Summary: A visit to her cousin Amy-Claire
helps five-year-old Rachel discover the joys of being a big sister.
ISBN 0-02-766991-2 [1. Sisters — Fiction. 2. Cousins — Fiction.]
I. Hamanaka, Sheila, ill. II. Title.
PZ7.M63963Vi   1992   [E] — dc20   91-280

To my friends on Spruce Avenue–C.M.

To my sister Lionelle–S.H.

*R*achel wished her father would drive faster. They were on their way from the airport to Amy-Claire's house.

Last year when Rachel visited her cousin Amy-Claire, the girls swung on a tire hung from a tree. They took bubble baths together and used up a whole bottle of bubbles. They made report cards for each other, with A's and B's and F's. Rachel could hardly wait to do all those things again.

Amy-Claire was seven, two years older than Rachel. She knew everything. Not like Rachel's little sister, Jessie. Jessie was only two. She didn't know anything.

In her car seat next to Rachel, Jessie was scribbling—in Rachel's coloring book. She was singing as she scribbled—Rachel's favorite song.

"London Bridge! Bridge! Bridge!" Jessie sang, loudly and off-key.

Rachel poked her to be quiet.

"Rachel poked me!" Jessie shouted.

"Here we are," Rachel's father said.

They pulled into Amy-Claire's driveway. There was Amy-Claire's house. And there on the front steps stood Uncle Jim and Aunt Susan and Amy-Claire.

As soon as her father turned off the engine, Rachel raced across the lawn. "Amy-Claire! Amy-Claire! Can we swing on your tire? Right now?"

"Maybe later," Amy-Claire said. "Ooh, Jessie," she squealed. "You're so cute! Can I hold her, Aunt Cindy, can I? I'll be real careful. Please!"

Rachel stared. Who would want to hold Jessie? Jessie was heavy. The front of her dress was purple from spilled grape juice.

Jessie stretched out her arms to Amy-Claire. "Hold me," she said.

Rachel followed them into the house. "Can we take a bubble bath after supper?"

Amy-Claire made a face. "I don't take baths anymore," she said. "I take showers."

"Bath!" Jessie said. "Rub-a-dub dub dub dub dub . . ."

"I'll give you a bath," Amy-Claire told Jessie. "With lots and lots of bubbles."

"Amy-Claire, can we make report cards later, like we did last time?" Rachel asked. "I'll put all A's on yours." Jessie couldn't make report cards. She was too little.

"I don't want to play school," Amy-Claire said. "I want to play house. I'll be the mother, and Jessie can be my baby. Right, Jessie?"

"Right," Jessie echoed.

Playing house with Jessie! Rachel felt like getting into the car and driving back home.

Amy-Claire and Jessie played house for a whole hour. Amy-Claire pushed
Jessie around in the stroller. She found an old bottle, and Jessie lay on the
grass, sucking away as if she hadn't given up the bottle for good at Christmas.
Rachel watched them from the screened porch.
"Why don't you play, too?" Mother asked her.
"I don't want to," Rachel said.

For dinner at noon, there was roast beef with mashed potatoes and gravy. Last time, Amy-Claire had shown Rachel how to make her mashed potatoes into a volcano, with gravy running down the sides like molten lava.

This time Amy-Claire begged, "Aunt Cindy, can I feed Jessie?"

"Jessie feeds herself," Mother said.

"No!" Jessie shouted. "Claire feed me."

"Okay, Jessie. Open wide," Amy-Claire said. "Here's the mashed potato airplane, coming in for a landing."

Rachel hoped it would crash.

At least Jessie took a nap after lunch. Rachel thought naps were the best thing ever invented.

While Jessie slept, Rachel and Amy-Claire took turns swinging on the tire swing.

They picked dandelions.

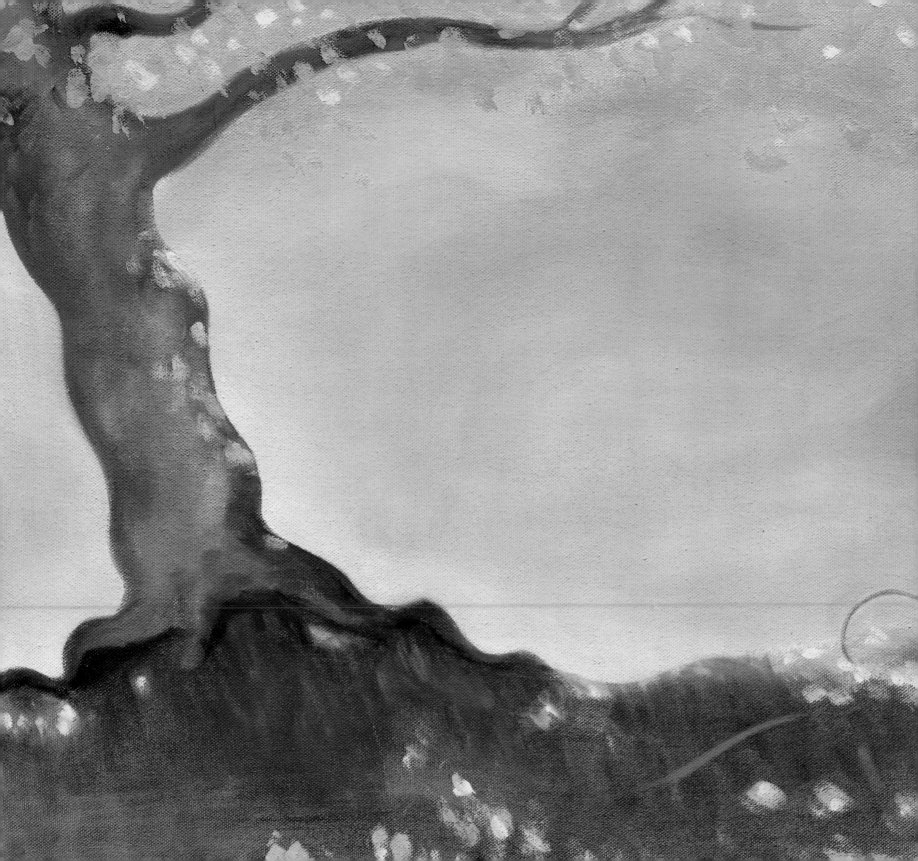

They put on bathing suits and sprayed each other with Amy-Claire's hose.

Then Jessie woke up.

"Baby Jessie!" Amy-Claire pounced on her. "Let's pretend that you're sick. You have an ear infection. Oh, my poor, sick baby!"

Rachel stomped back to the porch. She hoped Amy-Claire would call after her, *Rachel, please stay! Jessie, go away. I want to play with Rachel.* But Amy-Claire didn't.

Amy-Claire pretended to take Jessie's temperature with a Popsicle stick.

Rachel picked at a hole in the toe of her sneaker.

Amy-Claire covered Jessie with a towel. They were laughing together.
Rachel closed her eyes and sucked the end of her pigtail.

Then she lay face-down on the wicker couch and put a pillow over her head. With her eyes closed, she counted to sixty, hoping that sixty more seconds had gone by.

Finally she made herself open her eyes and go back outside. Jessie was lying in the hammock, pretending to be sick. Amy-Claire was rocking her and singing a lullabye.

"Are you still playing ear infection?" Rachel asked.

Amy-Claire nodded.

Rachel swallowed hard. "Can I be something?"

"You can't be the doctor," Amy-Claire said. "I already took Jessie to the doctor. Do you want to be the father?"

Rachel shook her head. Girls weren't fathers. But she wanted to be something.

Suddenly Rachel had an idea. "I could be the big sister," she said.

Amy-Claire had been having fun all day acting like a big sister to Jessie. Last time she had acted like a big sister to Rachel. Maybe a big sister wasn't such a bad thing to be.

"You're lucky," Amy-Claire said. "You really are a big sister. I wish I was."

Lucky? But Rachel knew Amy-Claire was right.

"Later let's show Jessie how to swing on the tire," Rachel said to Amy-Claire. "And how to make report cards. And how to take a bath all full of bubbles. Okay?"

"Okay," Amy-Claire said. "But now lie down and be sick! If you're the big sister, then you have an ear infection, too."

Rachel climbed into the hammock. Jessie cuddled up next to
her, sticky from spilled fruit punch, but soft and warm, too. It
felt nice lying next to her very own little sister.

"On the way home I'll teach you the words to London
Bridge," Rachel whispered to Jessie.

"Bridge! Bridge!" Jessie echoed, snuggling closer.